Just you
wait, Winona!

Look out for more Definitely Daisy titles

You're a disgrace, Daisy!
You must be joking, Jimmy!
I'd like a little word, Leonie!
Not now, Nathan!
What's the matter, Maya?
Dream on, Daisy!

Just you wait, Winona!

Jenny Oldfield

Illustrated by
Lauren Child

*Hodder
Children's
Books*

a division of Hodder Headline Limited

A Catalogue record for this book is available from
the British Library

ISBN 0 340 78499 7

Printed and bound in Great Britain

Hodder Children's Books
a division of Hodder Headline Ltd
338 Euston Road
London NW1 3BH

One

'And Daisy Morelli is going for the World Handstand Record!'

Leonie Flowers used her fist as a microphone. She commentated on Daisy's attempt to cross the playground on her hands.

'Yes, she's pacing herself perfectly, going strongly down the final stretch...!' Leonie's voice rose with excitement.

'Watch out, Nathan!' Jimmy Black cleared Daisy's path, getting all the kids to shoo out of her way.

Daisy felt the blood rush to her head so that her eyes practically popped out of their sockets. Her wrists ached, her arms shook, but she gritted her teeth and walked bravely on.

'And now she only has ten metres to go!' Leonie gabbled, reaching fever-pitch. 'Will she make it...? (Get off the official World Record Track, Winona!) This magnificent athlete is staggering a little as the effort begins to tell...

'But if Morelli succeeds in this attempt, it'll go down in the history of sport as one of mankind's greatest achievements...!'

Daisy's legs swayed and wobbled in mid-air. She saw everything upside-down: the playground wall, kids' feet and legs, Winona Jones's neat, black patent leather shoes.

'Daisy, stop that at once. You'll do yourself an injury!'

Winona doubled forward so that her blonde curly hair and smooth pink face appeared in Daisy's line of vision.

'Get-out-of-my-way!' Daisy grunted. Eight metres, seven metres, six metres to go. Would her arms last out?

Winona was still there. 'The blood will all rush to your head... you'll get blisters on your hands... Daisy Morelli, I can see your belly-button!'

Grunt-grunt. Five metres to go. Daisy's legs felt as heavy as lead. But the whole of Woodbridge Junior was watching this attempt and she refused to give in.

Dong-dong-dong! Daisy heard something that sounded like a playground bell explode inside her head. Oh no; she'd had a brain seizure from being upside down for too long. She'd overdone it, like Winona warned. This was it... the end! She sagged and sank to the ground.

'Aah!' Maya, Kyle, Jared and Jade sighed as the record attempt failed. 'Nearly! Yeah, that's a shame. Pity Winona had to go and ring the stupid bell!'

Finding her brain still in one piece inside her skull and her blood still pumping normally, Daisy opened her eyes.

And there was Winona-Stupid-Jones standing over her, playground bell in hand, saying with a smirky-smile, 'Oh, sorry, Daisy. Did I make you jump?'

* * *

'Have you seen your hair lately?' Winona asked, standing in front of Daisy later that morning in the queue for the school photographer.

Daisy ignored her. After what Winona had done during her world record attempt, she had sworn in public, surrounded by Jimmy and the rest of the gang, never to speak to Winona again.

'Your hair's a complete mess,' Winona advised, overlooking the fact that Daisy had ignored her. 'Here, would you like to borrow my brush?'

Winona's own blonde curls were in perfect order.

The queue shuffled forward as Maya took her place in front of the camera and smiled shyly into the lens.

'Just you wait, Winona!' Daisy muttered under her breath, forgetting her earlier oath. She glared at the hairbrush, then deliberately mussed up her long, dark hair some more.

'You've got felt-tip marks all down the front of your shirt,' Winona pointed out primly, dipping into her pocket and offering Daisy her spare school tie to cover up the mess.

I'd like to strangle you with that! Daisy thought darkly.

Jimmy's turn to face the camera had arrived. Daisy watched her best friend try to push his floppy brown hair back from his forehead in a failed attempt to tidy himself up. Then he stepped

forward like a soldier in front of the firing-squad, chin jutting, teeth clenched.

'Say sausages!' the photographer ordered.

'Sausages!'

Jimmy flinched as the camera clicked.

'Next!'

And Leonie took Jimmy's place, laid back as always, her black curly hair in a neat halo around her face, a wide smile and big, shiny brown eyes.

'Say sausages!'

'Saus-age-(*click*)-s.'

'Good. Next!' The busy photographer kept the kids coming.

It was Nathan Moss's turn. He took his place, complete with Legs, his pet spider.

Legs perched on Nathan's shoulder, happy to have his photograph taken.

The man behind the camera focused. 'Say saus... Good Lord, what on earth's that?' He sprang back to a safe distance, staring in horror at Nathan's fat black pet.

'This is Legs,' Nathan said, matter-of-factly.

'He's perfectly harmless.'

To prove the point, Legs stretched each of his eight legs and took a stroll around the back of Nathan's neck, to reappear confidently on the other shoulder.

'Sweet!' Leonie whispered brightly as she passed by Daisy and Winona still waiting in the queue. They were all used to weird Nathan and his unusual pet.

But she happened to catch Winona making an attack with her hairbrush on an unwilling Daisy's tangled hair. And Leonie shot Daisy a puzzled look, running to catch up with Jimmy and whisper in a loud voice, 'Since when did Daisy make friends with Winona Jones?'

Jimmy shrugged and glanced back at the two girls in the queue.

'I didn't!' Daisy hissed hotly. She wished with all her heart that she could get Miss Perfect out of her hair. Literally.

But Jimmy and Leonie didn't hear. First a failed record attempt, now this. Daisy knew that her reputation had hit an all-time low.

'Daisy Morelli, she ees, 'ow you say, ze traitor!' Standing daydreaming in the photographer's queue, Daisy pictured a dark underground tunnel; probably a sewer under the streets of Paris. Jimmy and Leonie were resistance fighters during the Second World War, which they'd just finished watching a video about in history.

'Nev-aire!' Jimmy's face went pale with shock. 'Thees Daisy, she is our number one agent. 'Ow can she be ze enemy?'

The black sewer dripped and gurgled as Leonie convinced Jimmy that Daisy, their leader, had indeed changed sides.

'...It's a lie!' Daisy declared when Jimmy and Leonie finally cornered her in a slimy,

rotting corner of the sewers and faced her, pistols in hand. 'I swear I never wanted to even speak to Winona Jones, never mind let her comb my hair!'

Leonie and Jimmy had refused to listen...
'Next!' the photographer barked from his position behind the camera.
The portrait-taker had dealt hastily with

Nathan and Legs, then moved on to Winona.

Winona stepped into position with a well-rehearsed smile. Her tie was neatly knotted, her white collar spotless.

'Sausages!' she said without prompting.

Click. 'Perfect! Next!'

Daisy sat down in front of the lens in a foul mood. Her street-cred was nil, thanks to

Winona, who, besides ruining her reputation with Jimmy, Leonie and the rest, had spoiled her best chance yet of winning the hand-stand record.

So she scowled at Winona's neat rear-view, wondering how on earth she could get her own back.

'Say...' the photographer began.

'Sausages!' Daisy snarled, all teeth and spit. And when Miss Ambler handed over the photos to take home at the end of the day, all Daisy's friends laughed at hers.

Daisy blushed then scowled at her image. No way would her mum and dad want to buy this snarling, snapping portrait.

'You look like a mad dog with rabies,' Winona giggled from her seat next to Daisy. Her own photograph had turned out chocolate-box perfect, of course.

Daisy shoved the horrid picture into her bag, alongside Herbie, her beanie-babe hamster. She pretended not to care, even when Winona insisted on tagging along with her to coo-coo over Daisy's baby sister, Mia, at the school gate.

But inside, she was boiling, fuming, furious. Smoke was coming out of her ears, she was plotting horrible accidents for Winona by fire, flood and earthquake.

'Goo-goo!' Winona stooped to play with Mia's pink rabbit.

'See you tomorrow, Jimmy!' Daisy called out as he passed by with the usual gang – Leonie, Maya, Jared and co.

Her best mate hardly bothered to reply. Instead, Jared passed a secret remark and they all laughed like crazy.

Standing next to Winona, Mia and her mum, Daisy felt snubbed, cut out, cold-shouldered and alone.

'Choo-choo-chobble!' the blonde super-pupil gurgled beside her.

'Goo-goo-ca-choo!' Mia burbled back.

In her mind, Daisy was tossing up Winona's savage fate.

She forced the glamorous blonde enemy to the rim of an active volcano. Molten lava smoked and bubbled redly only feet below. Within seconds Winona Jones would be no more...

Two

'Rain, rain, rain!' Daisy's dad punched and thumped pizza-dough on a floury board.

Outside the Pizza Palazzo on a typical English Saturday in June the raindrops bounced off the pavement.

'They call this summer!' Gianni gave a rich, deep laugh. 'But here in England there is no sun, no one is smiling. Only rain!'

Daisy stood nearby in a red striped apron,

waiting for her dad to hand her a chunk of dough. The smell of cooking pizzas wafted around the restaurant and out on to Duke Street.

'Hey, Daisy, what are you doing here?' Angie Morelli emerged from the wine cellar in the basement. 'How come you're not off playing with the gang?'

''Cos no one bothered to call for me, that's why not.'

Daisy's black mood of the day before had deepened. When Gianni tossed her a fistful of bendy dough, she slapped it on to the board and battered it flat. *Die, die!*

'Hey, you want to kill this pizza or cook it?' her dad protested, slapping his own chunk of dough lightly and niftily between his broad palms.

'So where's Jimmy today?' Angie asked, stacking bottles into the wine rack. Soon the restaurant would be crowded with hungry weekend shoppers wanting lunch.

'Dunno,' Daisy muttered. Don't care.

'And Leonie?'

'Dunno.' *Hammer-hammer-bash*.

'Hmm.' Her mum was just beginning to feel sorry for her when she saw a figure with a red umbrella struggle through the doorway. 'Ah, never mind,' she said brightly. 'Here comes Winona to keep you company!'

No, please, no! Daisy bashed her dough so hard that she made a hole right through the middle. Her dad picked up the sorry grey object between his thumb and forefinger and tutted in dismay. 'Daisy mia, in Italy they put you in prison for making pizza this way!'

'Hi everyone!' Winona chirped. She shook her wet umbrella then snapped it shut. 'Mrs Morelli, I just happened to be passing and I wondered if you'd like me to look after Mia for a while.'

'How nice!' Angie smiled gratefully. 'Thanks, Winona, but Mia's having her morning nap right now.'

'So come help make pizzas,' Gianni

invited. He unhooked a spare apron and showed Winona what to do.

Soon Ms TV Cook of the Year was flipping and twizzling dough like a pro.

'Excellent!' Gianni beamed. 'You want a job making pizza, Winona; you come to Pizza Palazzo any time!'

Winona smiled and blushed modestly at her success.

Sidelined in her own family kitchen, Daisy glared. She was halfway through trying a second time with a fresh piece of dough, making the same sulky botch as before, when the door opened again.

'Hi, Mr Morelli, Hi, Mrs Morelli!' Jimmy piped. He came in carrying his football as always, and wearing his blue-and-white football strip. At first he didn't spot Daisy and Winona working behind the counter.

Leonie and Jared burst in after him. 'We came to see if Daisy wants to play footie...' Leonie tailed off when she caught sight of the two busy cooks.

Daisy was doing her best to vanish. Her face was splodged with flour, her fingers sticky with pizza-dough. She even had clumps of it in her hair.

Winona didn't have a stray speck of flour anywhere. 'Hi, everyone!' she chirped. 'It's raining, in case you hadn't noticed!'

'So?' Leonie frowned. She looked suspiciously from Winona to Daisy, then back again.

Winona was nine-going-on-ninety. 'So the park will be muddy.

'You can hardly play football when the weather's like this!'

'Caught red-handed!' That evening, Daisy consoled herself by confiding in Herbie.

The one-eyed beanie-babe hamster listened quietly. He lay squidged on her duvet, thinking things through.

'I mean, how unlucky can you be!' Daisy went back through the day. 'There I am, innocently helping Dad when Winona shows up. I never asked her, did I? I can't help it if she barges into my life, can I?'

Herbie considered the problem carefully.

'The thing is, Herbie, it looks bad. Jimmy and Leonie think I've made friends with the teacher's pet on purpose. Like, yeah!' She spread her hands, palms upwards. 'Me, Daisy Disaster-Morelli make friends with Winona-Perfecta Jones!

'Crazy, huh?'

'Daisy, stop talking to yourself and go to sleep!' Angie put her head around the door. 'It's half-past ten!'

Daisy waited until her mum closed the door and went away. 'So anyway, I'm meant to be the leader of the gang. Well, not the leader exactly, but I'm the one with good ideas usually.

'Like, Herb, you remember the trouble I went to when Miss Ambler confiscated you that time I took you into assembly?

'It was *my* idea to get Leonie to ask to look in the teacher's locked cupboard for her so-called missing pencil-case. Then Maya had to deliberately spill orange juice all over Roald Dahl to drag Miss Boring-Snoring away so that I could sneak up and grab you out of the cupboard when she wasn't looking...' Daisy paused for breath, while Herbie looked faintly bored.

'*Sleep*, Daisy!' Angie was passing along the landing again and heard the chuntering still going on inside Daisy's room.

Daisy sighed and fidgeted under her bedclothes. 'Anyway, the point is, Winona's gone and ruined all that by hanging around me when I don't even ask her. She sticks like glue and I can't bear it. I mean, when I saw Jimmy coming out of his place at teatime, he never even stopped to ask me if I wanted to play footie! Think about it!'

She was so upset at the memory that she didn't notice when her beanie hamster slid down the duvet and over the edge of the bed. He landed with a soft thud on the floor.

'So what am I gonna do?' Daisy whined. 'I mean, Herbie, what would you do in my situation? ...Herbie? ...Herb?'

Silence from the hamster.

'Oh great!' she muttered. 'Now even my own hamster is refusing to talk to me!'

Sunday was sunny. Ideal park weather. And no one called.

All during breakfast Daisy waited for Jimmy to show. She punctured the soft yolk of her poached egg and mopped up every last drop with fingers of toast, kidding herself that it was still early, that soon Jimmy's knock would come and he'd be standing there in his blue-and-white kit, asking her to play.

'Why are you moping around in the house on a lovely sunny morning?' her mum asked, whisking away Daisy's plate and glass.

'I don't feel like going out,' Daisy grunted, twiddling a strand of hair and staring gloomily out of the window.

'In that case, why don't you entertain Mia for half an hour while I pop out for a newspaper?' Angie suggested.

Daisy jumped up from the table, stuck her feet into her trainers and shot out of the door. 'Sorry, Mum. I just remembered I said I'd meet Maya...'

Zoom! She was downstairs and out of the door before her mum drew breath.

And now that she was out on the sunny street, she felt more like her usual self.

There were walls to walk along, puddles

from yesterday to jump in or over, red men to stop at crossings for and green men to go.

And there was the pet-shop window to stare in, baby rabbits to coo over, a parrot on a stick outside the door to talk to.

'Where's Molly?' the yellow-and-white bird croaked. 'Molly, Molly, Molly! She's my girl!'

Daisy jumped back, then grinned. 'He-llo!' she croaked back in what she thought was a parrot-voice.

'Where's Molly?' The parrot ducked its head then twitched it from side to side. It spread its bright yellow comb of feathers until they stuck up punk-style on top of its head.

'He-llo!' Daisy cooed.

'Molly, Molly, Molly! She's my girl!'

'That's a great conversation you're having there!' Leonie Flowers happened to be passing by, on her way to the park.

Daisy dropped her new friend the parrot and seized her chance to join Leonie. 'Hey,' she said casually.

'Hey,' Leonie replied. She allowed Daisy to

walk down the street with her, half-pretending that she wasn't there.

'He-llo!' the parrot called after them.

Daisy and Leonie paused, then grinned over the bird's bad timing.

'So, you coming to play footie?' Leonie wanted to know.

Daisy beamed with relief. Despite the Winona disaster, things in the gang were OK after all. 'Who gets to choose teams?' she asked as they trotted through the park gates together.

Daisy and Leonie were hot and sticky, tired and thirsty when they flopped down on their backs under the horse chestnut tree after the hard fought match.

'Three-ee – two, three-ee – two!' Jared and Jimmy crowed as they went off arm in arm.

'We *let* you win!' Daisy shouted after them. 'But next time, don't count on us being so nice!'

The boys swaggered on regardless.

'Good game, so I don't mind losing,' Leonie

sighed, staring up at the pattern of green leaves against the blue sky.

For a while Daisy let a contented silence develop. Then she broke it with the question that had been bugging her since Friday.

'Leonie, what am I gonna do about Winona Jones?'

She'd thought carefully before raising the subject. Winona wasn't a topic you brought up lightly, since it could easily spoil the mood of the moment. But Daisy knew she could trust Leonie.

Reasons: 1) Leonie could sometimes run faster than Jimmy. 2) Leonie liked Legs. 3) Leonie and Daisy were on the same wavelength about schoolwork (ie. they both did as little as possible).

The list could have been longer, because the better Daisy got to know Leonie, the more she admired her.

For instance, Leonie didn't even have to try in order to succeed. Her long legs made her easily the best athlete in the school. In Art, she could take a piece of chicken wire and a bag of plaster and make a lifelike horse sculpture out of it in a single lesson. ('All by herself, with only a little advice from me!' Miss Ambler would boast to the school inspector.) This could have made Leonie a teacher's pet like Winona, but didn't.

Because the best thing about Leonie Flowers, and the quality which Daisy most envied in her, was that she had perfected the art of being naughty without *ever* getting into trouble.

So, when Daisy flopped under the tree and asked, 'Leonie, what am I gonna do about Winona Jones?', she expected sound advice.

The-girl-most-likely-to-succeed thought for a while. 'Well, you can't exactly stop her from trying to be your friend.'

Daisy acknowledged this. 'I know, I tried that. It doesn't work.'

Winona kept on popping up in her shiny black shoes, charming the pants off Daisy's parents.

Leonie thought some more, then came up with a brainwave.

'What you have to do is convert her. Make her change.'

Hmm, interesting. 'You mean, stop her from being Miss Ambler's pet and turn her into one of us?'

Leonie nodded. 'No more Saint Winona.'

Yeah! Daisy took the point. She admired Leonie's brilliant mind. 'Make her as bad as possible so she can join the gang? If we can get her into trouble and turn her into one of us, then end of problem!'

'Exactly!' Leonie rolled over on to her stomach to point out to Daisy that the subject of their conversation had just walked through the park gates with her pet poodle, Lulu.

Winona walked her dog at a distance. She carefully avoided yesterday's puddles and kept dainty Lulu on her nice red lead. The sun shone on her golden hair, fastened neatly into place with silver clasps.

'Hmm, could be difficult,' Daisy murmured. Winona was hardly a natural rebel. In fact, she was born to please.

'Yeah,' Leonie agreed, narrowing her dark brown eyes.

Winona the Good had never been told off in her entire life.

'Difficult but possible.'

Daisy nodded. 'What we need now is a carefully worked out plan,' she said.

Three

'La-la, la-la-la!'

Winona Jones trilled a bright tune at Midge the school hamster.

Midge chomped hard on the scoop of grain and nuts which the pet-monitor had just tipped into her bowl. She puffed out her fat little cheeks and stored food for later – *stuff-stuff, munch-munch*.

It was Monday morning – and the start of

the No-More-Saint-Winona project.

'Thank you for remembering to feed Midge, Winona dear.' Miss Ambler said, walking into the classroom with the register tucked under her arm.

'That's OK, Miss,' Winona replied in her sing-song voice.

'And please, Miss Ambler, may I clean out her cage at playtime?'

Leonie stole a glance at Daisy and made sick-noises.

'It's only because it's raining and she wants to stay in during morning break!' Daisy hissed.

But frumpy Miss Ambler in her flat shoes and frilly blouse was completely taken in by the Saint Winona routine. 'Of course you may, dear. Oh, and while I'm thinking about Midge, I've chosen you, Winona, to take her home and look after her during Spring Bank Holiday.'

'Miss, that's not fair!' Jade protested from her seat at the back of the room.

'Miss, we usually put our names in a box and the teacher draws one out,' Nathan patiently explained the process by which these things were done. He felt sorry for Miss Ambler because she was struggling towards the end of her first year in teaching.

'Winona did it last time!' Kyle Peterson pointed out.

'Not fair, not fair, not fair...' The low chorus rumbled around the room.

'La-la, la-la, la-la-la!' Winona hummed away with a smug smile.

'Children!' Miss Ambler put on her disapproving face and voice. With her head to one side and wearing a frown, she explained her bare-faced favouritism. 'Winona is my pet-monitor for the summer term, and she's been so good at her job that I've decided to reward her by letting her take Midge home again.'

'Not-fair-not-fair-not...' Rebellion rumbled on as the teacher plumped down at her desk and began to read names from the register.

For once, Daisy didn't join in the protests. Let Winona enjoy her moment of glory, she thought, since this is likely to be the last one she'll have for quite a while! Like, ever!

Sitting across the aisle in her seat by the window, Leonie caught Daisy's eye and nodded.

The Grand Plan, as agreed by Daisy and Leonie under the horse-chestnut tree in the park, was about to begin.

Step one: Miss Ambler would hand the completed register over to Saint Winona to take to the office as usual. (Besides being pet-monitor, Winona was also register monitor.)

Step two: Daisy would slip out at the same time, for some made-up reason. ('Please, Miss, I need the loo!'/ 'Miss Ambler, can I fetch Herbie from my coat pocket?'/ 'Miss, I forgot my packed lunch. May I go to the office and phone my mum?')

Step three: Daisy would waylay Winona and offer to take the register to Mrs Hannam for her. Even Winona would be happy to give up this boring job and make a speedy return to the classroom.

Step four: Daisy would deliberately "forget" to deliver the register to the office. Mrs Hannam would panic. The whole school would be thrown into chaos by the hunt for Miss Ambler's class register. The register would later be "found", dusty and bashed, behind a radiator in the assembly hall by Leonie.

Outcome: Winona would get the blame for failing to deliver the register as instructed. No one would believe her when she claimed she'd handed over the register to Daisy Morelli of all people.

Major disgrace. Mega loss of saintliness. Winona would be in the teacher's bad books for the first time in her entire life.

Steps One and Two went perfectly.

Winona and Daisy emerged from the classroom into the corridor at exactly the

same time. ('Use the packed-lunch excuse.'
Leonie had recommended. 'That one always
works with Ambler!') Step Three also went
the way it should.

'I'll take that!' Daisy seized the register
from Winona and gave her a cheesy smile.

'How come?' Winona was suspicious.

' 'Cos I'm going to the office to make a
phone call in any case. Why don't you nick
off to the cloakroom for a couple of minutes?'
(*Go comb your hair, polish your halo, why
don't you?*)

Winona smiled back. 'OK, Daisy, thanks a
lot. See you.' She scooted off down the
corridor, innocently free of her duty.

It was Step Four where the problems
occurred.

Daisy had the class register in her hot little
hands. Now she had to stuff it down the
back of the radiator in the hall, for Leonie to
discover later.

So she snuck quietly past Mrs Hunt's
classroom, hunched down so that no one

could see her. Then she took a right turn into the assembly hall.

Tiptoe-tiptoe towards the chosen radiator, which was in the corner where the P.E. equipment was stored.

Daisy held her breath as she clambered over long benches and rolled-up rubber mats. If anyone saw her now, right this moment, she'd be in deep trouble...

'Sorry, no can do!' Mrs Hunt's classroom door opened and clicked shut again as Bernie King, the school caretaker, emerged into the corridor. As usual he was telling the teacher why he didn't have time to mend her window blind. 'I've got too much on; benches to set out for assembly, for a start!'

Oh no, not Bernie King! Daisy slithered off the mats, then ducked down behind the piano which was stashed away behind the P.E. benches. He would be with his black-and-white bulldog, Lennox, and, by the sound of the caretaker's jangling keys, the two of them were heading for the hall!

Pitter-pat, pitter-pat! The squat dog's claws rattled against the shiny red lino-tiles. Lennox the Bruiser, Lennox the wheezy, bad-breath heavyweight who waddled everywhere at his master's heels.

Clutching the register tight to her chest, Daisy squatted low behind the piano.

'Teachers!' Bernie King muttered as he entered the hall and made a bee-line for the benches. 'They must think I've got nothing to do all day!'

Huh-a, huh-a, huh! Lennox breathed hard and sniffed at the rubber mats.

'Down, boy!' Bernie commanded, lifting the first bench ready to set it out for assembly.

Sniff-sniff-sniff! Lennox scaled the mat mountain.

Daisy could hear the dog's hot breath wheezing noisily at the side of the piano. Then his white face appeared, jaws drooling, little pink eyes homing in on her.

Wrr-ooo-ff! Half-growl, half-bark, Lennox gave a ferocious noise that made Daisy jump out of her skin.

Shaking from head to foot, she stood up.

'What the...?' Bernie came over to investigate.

'Daisy Morelli, what the dickens are you doing there with that register?'

'I know, Mr King, I know!' Sorrowfully Miss Ambler shook her head and frowned at Daisy. The caretaker and his dog had frog-marched the hideaway out of the hall, down the corridor and back to the classroom.

Bernie was in full flow. 'I might've guessed who it was skulking behind that piano!' he insisted. 'I don't know what it is about this particular girl, but somehow whenever there's trouble, I expect Daisy Morelli to be in the thick of it!'

Miss Ambler sighed and agreed.

Daisy stood in front of the whole class, kept at bay by a stern-looking Lennox. Her face burned with embarrassment.

When she snuck a glance around the room she could see Leonie with her gaze firmly fixed on the window, Jimmy looking worried for her, and Winona back at her desk looking pert and pink and squeaky-clean.

'If I were you I'd ask her what she was planning to do with that register!' King advised the rookie teacher. 'A register is an important official document. You can't just muck around and not take it to the office!'

'I know. I agree. Leave it with me,' Miss Ambler said, as firmly as she could.

So Bernie King went off grumbling, followed by a panting Lennox. And the teacher turned her attention to Daisy. 'Daisy Morelli, don't even try to explain!'

'Please, Miss...'

'I said, don't!'

'No, Miss.' Daisy did her best to look

upset, to work on the young teacher's soft side. Her dark hair fell forward to hide her face as she stared miserably at her shoes. Playing for sympathy was a long shot, but it might just work.

'It's one thing for Winona to agree to hand over the register when I'd sent her to the office with it...' Miss Ambler cast a sorrowful look in the direction of her star pupil. Winona's shiny smile faltered.

The teacher let Winona off the hook and turned back with a severe frown to the main culprit. 'But, Daisy, as Mr King quite rightly says, it's quite another for you to "muck around" with it in the assembly hall!'

'Yes, Miss.'

'And I don't even want to *know* what you planned to do with the register!' Miss Ambler's voice rose crossly as she glanced at her watch and saw that it was time for the class to file out to assembly.

'All I'm saying is that I agree with Mr King; if there's trouble in this school and we look around for the culprit, we never have to search far.

'Ask any one of the other teachers – Mrs Hunt, Mrs Waymann – who might be to blame and they all come up with the same answer. They don't even have to stop and think.

' "Who's the major troublemaker in Woodbridge Junior School?" Back comes the answer quick of a flash. "Daisy Morelli!" they tell me. "Yes, definitely Daisy!" '

Four

'OK, so the grand plan didn't work!' Leonie admitted.

She and Daisy managed to whisper a few words as they stood at the sink together, washing up paint materials after the art lesson.

'You can say that again,' Daisy moaned.

Not only had she been told off in front of the whole class – AGAIN! – but Winona had come out of the whole episode almost unharmed.

Worse still, Daisy's punishment was to stay in during every morning playtime this coming week!

('Why, Daisy; why?' Miss Ambler had sighed sadly over her naughty pupil. Then; 'No, don't tell me. I can't bear to hear your lame excuse!') 'So we have to think again!' Leonie insisted.

'Leonie Flowers, come away from that sink!' Miss Ambler ordered. 'Leave Daisy alone. It's time for you and the rest of the class to go out to play.'

Leonie managed a few final words without moving her lips.

Daisy noted yet another of Leonie's extraordinary talents.

'Like I say, we have to come up with another plan!' she hissed. (Actually, she said "another lan" since 'p' was impossible [*im-ossi-ul*] without moving her lips.)

'Leonie!' the teacher warned.

So Daisy's clever partner in crime dried her hands and went outside to snatch the world handstand record from her friend's grasp.

And Daisy herself took Herbie out of her drawer and sat with him in the corner of the classroom.

'We have to think of some other way of setting Winona up,' she said. 'So, any ideas?'

Herbie, hunkered on the window-sill, blinked back at her with his one beady eye.

Try letting Legs out of his jam-jar and claiming that it was Winona's fault. The hamster didn't speak out loud, but he was a whizz at telepathy.

Daisy's eyes lit up. 'Great idea!'

So she went straight across the empty classroom to look in Nathan's drawer.

Unfortunately, Nathan and his spider were like Bernie King and Lennox; they went everywhere together. It stood to reason; the jar would be empty and Legs would be out enjoying the fresh air with the school's resident weirdo.

As she was retreating to Herbie's corner to consult with him again, Daisy caught sight of Midge trundling inside the exercise-wheel in her cage at the opposite end of the window-ledge.

'So where's Miss Win-oh-na now?' she said out loud. 'I thought she was supposed to be cleaning you out this playtime!'

Midge didn't reply. She just trundled.

'Any more ideas?' Daisy asked Herbie, picking him up and stroking him thoughtfully.

You could try planting a valuable item in Winona's drawer, then claiming she stole it.

Phew! That was big-time badness. Daisy didn't know if she was up to that.

'What *kind* of valuable item?' she asked, puting Herbie down on the ledge closer to Midge's cage. 'You mean, like someone's watch or dinner-money?'

Herbie scrunched up his squidgy face into an unreadable expression.

'No, you're right; too risky!' Daisy agreed swiftly. She whizzed Herbie smoothly along the sill, making him collide gently with the live hamster's cage.

Thud! Herbie came to a skidding halt.

Inside the cage, Midge got down from her wheel and came to check out what was going on. She poked her whiskery golden face against the wire-mesh and scrabbled at it with her front paws.

'Sorry, Midge!' Daisy apologised for upsetting the school hamster. 'It was only me messing around with Herbie.'

Picking up the beanie toy, she showed him to Midge. 'See, he's a hamster like you. Only he's not the real live kind, worse luck...'

Daisy held her hamster beside Midge, who squeaked a warning for the soft toy to keep off her patch.

'It's OK, he can't...' Daisy began.

From down the corridor, she heard the
trip-trip-trip of dainty patent-leather shoes.
So Winona hadn't forgotten about cleaning
out Midge after all.

In the same moment, Daisy suddenly
noticed something important.

'Y'know, Herb; you and Midge look pretty
alike!' she whispered, staring from one to
the other. 'You're both a kind of faded,
fudgey-beige, not golden at all.

But I have only one eye, Herbie
reminded her.

'Yeah, yeah, forget that for a second. You're the same size and shape. In fact, you two could be twins!'

'Daisy, what are you doing?' Winona had opened the classroom door and marched forward with a challenge. 'It's my job to clean Midge out, as you very well know!'

'I'm not – I wasn't!' Quickly Daisy fumbled Herbie behind her back and stepped to one side.

Winona sniffed and tossed her curls. 'Anyway, I decided to do it tomorrow instead of today.'

Daisy hardly took any notice. All she could think about was the fact that Herbie and Midge looked like twins!

Of course, it was only the germ of an idea and Daisy would have to work it out properly with Leonie, but – wow – this could be good!

In fact, it was better than good.

'If this works, Miss Ambler will never trust Winona Jones ever again!' Admiration for

Daisy lit up Leonie's deep brown eyes.

' 'Course it'll work!' Daisy insisted.

She and Leonie had gathered in a huddle at the school gate first thing on Tuesday morning, along with Jimmy and Maya.

'So, run it by me.' Jimmy wanted to go over the plan yet again, ignoring the hordes of kids piling in through the gates.

Daisy went through events one more time.

'Our plan must be absolutely perfect,' the space station commander insisted to her tense crew. 'One small error will lead to total disaster!'

The three space travellers zipped up their silver suits and nodded nervously. They knew that their mission was important to the whole future of mankind.

Commander Morelli lowered her voice and spoke to each one in turn. 'Scott, your job is to fire the booster rockets at the right nano-second. Greg, you keep a lookout for alien ships. And Zed, you may only be a robot, but you're programmed to have feelings just like us humans. So if you come under too much pressure, you must hand over control of the weapon system to me. Understood...?'

'Got that!' Jimmy nodded as Daisy came to the end of the plan.

'OK, Maya?' Leonie checked. 'You think

you can remember to open the french-window next to your desk during the science lesson without Miss Ambler noticing?'

Their small, dark-haired accomplice nodded eagerly. 'I can't wait till playtime!' she grinned, then ran off, her long plait swinging down her back.

It was the same for Daisy, Leonie and Jimmy; the build-up to break churned up their stomachs and made them tense with excitement. None of them had ever known the morning tick forward so slowly. Miss Ambler and her science lesson had never been so boring-snoring.

Brrrring!

The bell for playtime startled Daisy. The teacher broke off and the pupils slammed their books closed. Everyone, including Jimmy, Leonie and Maya, scraped back their chairs and made a headlong dash for the door.

'Not you, Daisy Morelli!' Miss Ambler

shrieked above the noise. 'Your punishment was to miss every morning break this week, remember!'

'Yes, Miss Ambler,' Daisy said meekly.

So she stayed behind with Winona, who reminded Miss Ambler that her mission this playtime was to clean out Midge's cage.

'That's wonderful, dear,' the teacher murmured. 'It's so good of you not to mind giving up your break!'

So Winona waited until the classroom was empty except for Daisy, then she set to.

First she opened the hamster cage and lifted Midge out.

The fat little hamster squirmed in her cupped hands and wriggled as Winona carefully placed her inside the clear plastic ball which the school had bought specially.

The ball was about the size of a football and was made up of two halves which you unscrewed to open. The idea was to pop your pet hamster inside, screw the ball

back together and put it somewhere safe
while you cleaned the cage. Happy
hamster would meanwhile trundle about
contentedly inside the ball.

'There, Midge!' Winona cooed to the
disgruntled school pet as she set her on the
floor near to the door.

Midge was sulking about being inside
the ball. She squatted and refused to move
a muscle.

'So far, so good!' Daisy stayed in a far
corner of the room, but kept a careful eye
on what Winona was doing. Now it was
time, to quietly lift Herbie out of the corner
of her drawer where she'd kept him well-
hidden until he was needed.

Suddenly, as Winona got busy lifting the
old wood shavings out of the cage, there
was a loud rattle at the window.

'Hey, Winona!' Leonie knocked at the
pane furthest away from the french window
which led out into the playground. Her
voice was faint through the glass. 'Come

here a second!'

Winona scarcely looked up. 'Can't you see I'm busy?' she mouthed back.

'No, really; come over here!' Leonie acted as if she wanted to let Winona into a big secret. 'Kyle Peterson just told me he fancies you!'

'Ssshhh!' Wionona dropped the shavings and ran to join Leonie, tugging the window open. 'Yuck, Kyle Stupid Peterson! Do you want the whole school to know?' she asked crossly.

'Kyle fancies you; he honestly does!' Leonie said gleefully.

Her big "news" kept Winona occupied, as predicted.

Here was her chance! Daisy ran with Herbie to the spot on the floor where Winona had placed the plastic cleaning-ball.

Rapidly unscrewing it, she took out Midge and replaced her with the beanie lookalike.

Now everything depended on Maya.

Holding a squirming Midge, Daisy raced to the french window.

Would it be unlatched? Would Maya be there in the playground, waiting as planned?

Yes! Quickly Daisy opened the door and secretly slid Midge out to Maya. Then she dashed back to the ball with Herbie inside, took hold of it and set it rolling at high speed.

'Sorry, Herbie!' she whispered, as the ball disappeared out of the door.

'Hey, Winona!' she yelled immediately afterwards in an innocent, frightened voice. 'Winona, look out!'

'What?' Turning away from her enthralling conversation with Leonie about revolting Kyle Peterson, Winona was just in time to see the cleaning-ball vanish through the door. 'Oh!'

She squealed and put both hands over her mouth.

'Midge set her ball rolling!' Daisy cried.

'She ran like mad inside. Her little legs were going like fury!'

'Why didn't you stop her?' Winona asked faintly, panic rooting her to the spot.

'Me?' Daisy flung her arms wide. 'So it was my job to look after Midge, was it? Funny; as pet-monitor, I thought that was down to you!'

Winona gasped and geared herself for action. 'Don't just stand there!' she yelled at Daisy. 'Which way did Midge go?'

'To the left, down the ramp leading to the staffroom!' Daisy declared.

It was hard to keep a straight face as she stepped to one side to let Winona out of the door. This whole thing was working perfectly.

'Poor Midge!' Winona cried, completely taken in by the trick.

Then, 'Oh, no; if she trundles the ball past the staffroom, Miss Ambler might see the whole thing and think I've been careless. Then I'll be in terrible, terrible trouble!'

Five

'All I did was to ask Mr King if he would mind
mending the window blind in my classroom!'
Mrs Hunt sighed over her cup of coffee
during morning break. She was still cross
over the caretaker's refusal to help the
morning before.

'Bernie King is a law unto himself,' Miss
Ambler sympathized.

She sat opposite the open staffroom door,

gazing wearily into the corridor.

'As for his horrid, smelly dog...' Mrs Hunt moaned on.

'Good Lord!' Miss Ambler cut in. She put down her coffee and jumped to her feet.

'What is it?' Slower to react, the older teacher peered over her glasses in the direction of the open door.

'It was – no, it couldn't have been... there again, perhaps it could...!' Hesitating, stopping, then starting out into the corridor, Miss Ambler looked for the plastic hamster ball which, unless she'd been imagining things, had just trundled by.

Wumph! A frantic Winona Jones crashed into the puzzled teacher.

'Winona?' Miss Ambler took the full force of the blonde whirlwind chasing down the slope from the classroom. She dusted herself down then spoke severely. 'Correct me if I'm wrong, but wasn't that Midge I just saw rolling past the staffroom inside her cleaning-ball?'

Daisy could hardly keep the grin off her face.

She saw the crash between the teacher and her star pupil. She heard the tone of voice – "Correct me if I'm wrong..." Waiting a split second before she put in an appearance, she sprinted down the slope. Her hair flew back from her face, her shirt flapped out of the waistband of her skirt. 'Poor Midge!' she gasped, laying it on thick. 'Her little head must be spinning inside that ball!'

'Daisy!' Miss Ambler commanded her to stop. 'What's going on? How did the hamster get out into the corridor?'

'Miss, I can't stop. I have to catch up with Midge!' Daisy protested.

By this time the ball containing Herbie had reached a short flight of steps down into the playground.

Bounce-bounce-bounce! It vanished down the steps, through the door and out of sight.

'Yes, of course.' The teacher took her

point. 'Daisy, you carry on and bring the hamster back as fast as you can. Winona, you stay here. You and I need to have a little word!'

Brilliant! Superb! Excellent!

Daisy was busy congratulating herself and the whole gang.

Every detail had gone according to plan.

Space station commander to crew: All systems working perfectly. Repeat; all systems firing correctly. We're dead on course!

Relaxing now, she trotted down into the playground in time to see Jimmy in position, assuming a classic goalkeeper crouch.

He bent low, arms forward, palms wide, ready to catch the hamster cleaning-ball as it rolled across the tarmac towards him.

Trundle-trundle. The ball rattled and bumped over the hard surface. Inside, Herbie squidged and flopped against the clear sides. He looked for all the world like a dazed and dizzy, real live hamster.

'Oh, poor Midge!' kids gasped. The infants happened to be playing nearby and mistook the soft toy for the live animal.

One little boy from Reception Class cried loudly. 'Midge is dead!' he wept. 'I saw her, and she was all floppy!'

Ignoring all the kerfuffle, Daisy saw Jimmy crouch and wait until the last moment, then make a spectacular sideways dive.

'Good save!' Leonie cheered as Jimmy scooped up the ball.

'This way, Jimmy! Maya's waiting over by the bike shed!'

Perfect! Daisy jogged after Jimmy as he followed Leonie's directions.

Now all they had to do was complete the final stage of the plan.

Maya was waiting in the shed with Midge, as instructed. She had dashed with the hamster away from the french window, across the area of the playground marked out as a rounders pitch, and hidden away there until Daisy and Jimmy had carried out their parts.

Daisy had allowed one and a half minutes between swapping Herbie for Midge and this was the moment when all four plotters would meet up in the bike shed.

Another thirty seconds should see the second switch made.

Jimmy would hand the ball over to Daisy. Daisy would unscrew it and remove one crushed Herbie. Maya would pop Midge back into the ball. And while Leonie checked that the coast was clear, Daisy would screw the real hamster safe and sound back inside the cleaning-ball. Then the whole team would emerge and trot across the playground to loud cheers.

'Look, Daisy's gang saved Midge!'

'The hamster rolled all the way into the bike shed, wow!'

'I bet she's dizzy!'

'Winona Jones let her roll away!'

'Yeah, how dumb can you be?'

Daisy would carry Midge carefully on what would feel like a lap of honour.

Then she would re-enter the school building solo and climb the steps to the staffroom. Flushed and proud, she would present Midge to Miss Ambler.

And Winona would be... DEAD!

'OK, Maya, where's Midge?' Leonie asked breathlessly.

Jimmy and Daisy were just entering the shadowy bike shed and quickly unscrewing the plastic ball.

'Quick!' Jimmy gasped, holding out the empty ball. If they took too long over this phase, people might get suspicious.

Daisy grabbed Herbie and stuffed him into her shirt pocket, where he bulged fatly.

'Maya?' Leonie demanded. She noticed Maya's look of dismay, then glanced down at her empty hands. 'Where's Midge?'

The question made Daisy's blood run cold. Her fingers fumbled to tuck Herbie completely out of sight.

Jimmy held out the two halves of the cleaning-ball, waiting in vain.

'Where's Midge?' Jimmy, Daisy and Leonie repeated as one.

Maya's bottom lip wobbled. Tears appeared at the rims of her enormous dark eyes and caught in her long, thick lashes. And the explanation came out in a trembly voice, bit by bit.

'She wriggled,' Maya began.

'Yeah?' Leonie challenged.

Maya nodded. 'Her claws were sharp.'

'So?' Jimmy pushed.

'Then she bit me!' Maya held up a finger
to show them a bright red tooth-mark.

'You dropped her?' Daisy guessed. As
she said the words, she felt her whole
world collapse inwards like a deflated
hot-air balloon.

Sssssss. Her plan was rocking wildly, sinking fast.

Maya choked, then nodded. 'Midge escaped!' she admitted. 'I'm sorry, Daisy. I really am!'

Six

'This definitely wasn't meant to happen!' Daisy
felt like sagging to the ground and giving up.
Her beautiful plan lay in ruins.

But Leonie managed to keep it together.
'Where *exactly* were you when Midge
escaped?' she asked Maya.

'Over where Nathan is standing, by the
netball post.' Unable to meet their eyes, Maya
stood in the dark shed with eyes downcast, her

long black plait drooped over one shoulder.

'So let's go look!' Leonie set off at a jog, cruising around the netball pitch, eyes peeled for a small, furry, golden hamster.

For a second Jimmy carried on staring at the empty plastic ball in his hands. Then he drew a deep breath and dumped it on Daisy. 'Over to you!' he said, speeding after Leonie in search of runaway Midge.

'What are you looking for?' Nathan asked in a loud, suspicious voice.

'Back off, Nathan!' Leonie said quietly.

'Yeah, watch out!' Jimmy circled Nathan and his hairy, pot-bellied pet.

Legs stretched, then meandered down the length of Nathan's arm.

Under cover of the bike shed, Maya whispered to Daisy, 'What are we gonna do?'

Daisy shook her head. 'Can hamsters survive in the wild?' she asked.

Pictures of Midge cowering under a rose bush in someone's garden while the neighbourhood cat stalked round and round caught hold of Daisy's lively imagination.

A scared hamster trembling. A black cat prowling closer and closer, claws out, body ready to spring. Shiny green eyes piercing. A round, furry face frozen with fear. A little heart racing – until suddenly it sounded one final thump and gave out...

It could happen, Daisy knew. And she felt the black hand of guilt clutch at her own heart and take away her breath. 'This is all my fault!' she whispered, her face white with dread, hands shaking.

'What will we tell Miss Ambler?' Maya asked.

The bell for the start of lessons had just gone and the playground was emptying fast. Meanwhile, Jimmy and Leonie continued to cruise around the area where Midge had disappeared.

Daisy considered Maya's frightened question, then gave her reply. Tucking the empty plastic ball under one arm and squaring her shoulders, she marched towards the school. 'I'll confess!' she announced nobly. 'I'm gonna tell Miss

Ambler every single thing!'

'Not now, Daisy!' The teacher made it clear that she was too busy talking to Winona to listen.

With her friends around her, Daisy had held up the empty ball for all the class to see. She'd begun her full and frank confession. 'Midge escaped!'

A gasp had gone around the room. Everyone's gaze shot from the empty ball to the silent hamster cage in the corner.

Then Miss Ambler had cut her short. 'Can't you see that I'm trying to deal with Winona Jones? You'll have to wait!'

'B-b-but!' Daisy stammered.

'Yes, Daisy; I see that the hamster is missing. I'm not blind. I'm sure you, Maya, Leonie and Jimmy did your very best to stop it happening, and well done for trying. But now, just put the cleaning-ball on the window sill next to the cage and go and sit in your place.'

'W-w-we... I mean, I... I didn't mean for Midge to escape!' Daisy made what she thought was

a clean breast of it. She waited for the teacher's
angry response.

'No, Daisy, dear. None of us wanted to lose
our lovely little hamster. And I'm sure we all
know who to blame!' Miss Ambler shooed the
gang back to their seats, then returned to her
attack.

'I must say, Winona, that I'm very, *very*
disappointed in you!'

Standing at the front of the room, Winona
hung her head awkwardly but said nothing.

'I trusted you – the whole class trusted you –

to take good care of Midge. And what happened? A moment of pure carelessness when you turned your back and let her set the ball in motion, that's what happened!'

As Miss Ambler lectured hard, Daisy studied Winona's half-hidden face. She could see that she was red and trying not to cry. Even her blonde curls seemed to have drooped and lost their shine.

'One small careless action,' the teacher continued. 'But look at the result. Poor Midge is lost and we may never find her alive again!'

A shiver ran round the class. Someone on the front row sniffled quietly.

'I'm sorry, Miss Ambler,' Winona said in a tiny voice.

The teacher glared and delayed for maximum effect. Finally she delivered her verdict. 'On this occasion, Winona, I think I speak for everyone here when I tell you that sorry is not enough!'

'Well, our plan worked, didn't it?'

It was home-time and Leonie stood at the school gates pointing out the obvious to Jimmy, Maya and Daisy.

'Oh sure, it worked!' Jimmy said scornfully. 'Midge has only vanished, that's all!'

'I mean, we got Winona into Ambler's bad books, like we wanted,' Leonie insisted. 'She even had to go and see Waymann, remember!'

But Leonie's reminder fell strangely flat. Daisy recalled Winona's white, dull face as she'd trailed off to see the head teacher for one of her famous "little words". It was as if a bomb had dropped into Winona's world and left her shell-shocked.

Then, when she'd come back, Daisy had noticed with a rush of shame that Winona's eyes and nose were red from crying and she'd spent the rest of the afternoon with her head buried in the book she'd chosen from the library.

And now, after school, poor Winona was coming out of the building by herself, with no spring in her step, trying her best to avoid other kids from the class.

Poor Winona! Daisy pulled herself up short. *What am I saying; poor Winona*? Hadn't Miss Perfect made Daisy's own life a misery until now, with her unasked-for advice and superglue habit of sticking around where she wasn't wanted?

And now that the Midge incident had successfully pulled Winona down by several pegs, surely she would be less big-headed and goody-goody in future?

After all, that's the whole point! Daisy told herself firmly.

Poor Winona nothing! The hamster plot would all work out fine in the end. If only...

'If only we could find Midge!' Jimmy sighed, as if reading Daisy's thoughts.

Super-practical Leonie stepped in with a suggestion. 'Let's form a search party!'

'When?' Maya asked.

'Now!' Leonie shot back.

'Good idea,' Jimmy agreed.

So Leonie stood on the wall and asked for volunteers to stay behind and help find the missing hamster.

'Me; I will!' Jade offered, after checking with her big sister to see if it would be OK.

'Count me in,' Kyle piped up, giving Winona a sympathetic smile as she trailed by. 'How about you?' he asked her.

Winona shook her head. 'No, I have to go straight home or my mum will be worried,' she sighed.

Daisy felt another pang of guilt as she watched Winona leave, head bowed, patent-leather shoes scuffing slowly along the pavement. *Tomorrow!* she promised silently. *Tomorrow I'll confess everything to Miss Ambler!*

And by that time, with a bit of luck, they would have found Midge.

'I'd like to volunteer!' Nathan told Leonie. Which meant that Daisy, Jimmy, Leonie, Maya, Jade, Kyle and Nathan made up the search party.

'Where do we start?' Kyle asked, gazing around the vast playground. 'Where would Midge hide?'

'She could have scooted back into school,' Jade suggested.

'Hamsters like warm places.'

So Leonie told Jade and Kyle to search the entrance and the steps leading up to the staffroom. 'If Bernie King tries to chuck you out, tell him we're the official Midge search party and we've got permission to be in school.'

Kyle looked doubtful. 'Do we?'

'No. But Bernie won't know that, will he?' Leonie turned quickly to Maya and Jimmy. 'I think you two should check the bike shed.'

They nodded and sprinted across the yard.

'Daisy, you and I need to search outside the gates, along Woodbridge Road.' Leonie was in total charge now, thinking things through and positive that all would soon be well.

So Daisy fell in with her orders, until

Nathan stepped across their path and blocked their way.

'What about me?' he demanded, stony-faced. 'You didn't give me anything to do.'

'Oh, Nathan, right!' Leonie hesitated. What good would a geek like Nathan be, balancing along wall tops and peering into gardens? 'I know, you can go and join Kyle and Jade inside the building.'

Nathan stood his ground. His faded fair hair flopped over his forehead and stuck out at all angles from the top of his head, like he had a permanent electric shock. 'I'd rather be outside with you and Daisy,' he insisted.

'OK, but don't hold us back,' Leonie agreed, knowing there was no time to argue.

So the three of them set off down the street, stopping to ask the crossing-lady, then the man who owned the newsagents next door to the school. 'Did you see a runaway hamster earlier today by any chance?'

'No, sorry,' came the answer. Or, 'What does it look like... small, fat, fudge-coloured?

...No, sorry!'

Five minutes passed and they'd had no luck at all.

And it turned out that Nathan wasn't much help either. 'Waste of time asking these questions,' he mumbled, taking Legs out of his jam-jar and making tweeting noises at him with puckered lips. 'What we need to do is look for clues.'

'What *kind* of clues?' Daisy wanted to know. She and Nathan were waiting for Leonie, who had disappeared into yet another shop.

'Pawprints, droppings, that scientific kind of thing,' Nathan replied.

Daisy's jaw dropped. 'You're not serious!' How small were a hamster's pawprints? What chance did they have of spotting any on a stone pavement?

Nathan frowned. 'Deadly serious,' he insisted, thoughtfully stroking Legs. Then he pointed at the lumpy, squidgy, fudge-coloured object half poking out of Daisy's shirt pocket. 'Anyway, Daisy Morelli, why are you carrying Herbie around everywhere all squidged up like that?'

Seven

'Umm... er... um.' For once Daisy was lost for words.

Nathan narrowed his eyes behind the smudged lenses of his taped-up glasses. 'For a second you had me fooled into thinking that Herbie was Midge.'

'Ha! No way!' She felt a hot flush cover her whole body. Was Nathan's casual comment a fluke, or did he know something?

The school boffin continued his weirdly accurate train of thought. 'I mean, Herbie and Midge do look alike. It would be easy to mistake one for the other...'

'Like, yeah!' Daisy did her best to scoff. 'Only *you* would think that, Nathan!'

Luckily Leonie came out of the shop just at that moment. She held up a bar of nut chocolate. 'I bought this to tempt Midge out of hiding,' she explained. 'I think it's time we went back to school and re-grouped.'

So the three of them re-traced their steps along Woodbridge Road, still searching under hedges and in litter bins as they went along, asking anyone who would listen if they had seen a runaway hamster.

No – No – No. The answer was always the same.

'Well, that was a complete waste of time,' Nathan said, as they ran back through the school gates.

'No need to sound so smug,' Leonie grumbled.

Yeah, Nathan, Daisy thought. *How come you're not the least bit worried about what happened to Midge?* She didn't say anything, but her questions about the strange boy's attitude were mounting. For instance, why had he offered to join the search party if he couldn't care less about the hamster? And why was he grinning secretly to himself as Jimmy and Maya came trotting across the playground to inform Leonie that there was no sign of Midge in the bike shed?

'Out!' a voice boomed from inside the school.

Jimmy, Maya, Daisy, Leonie and Nathan swung round just in time to see Kyle and Jade charging down the stone steps. They tripped and tumbled over themselves in their haste.

'The King has spoken!' Leonie recognised the hand of the grumpy caretaker behind the rapid exit.

And sure enough, the squat figures of Bernie King and Lennox soon appeared in the doorway. Man and dog loomed over the two quivering kids.

'Who gave you permission to come snooping round school after the bell's gone?' Bernie demanded, folding his thick arms and filling up the entire door frame.

Wrrroooff! Lennox lent his support. His jowls slavered, his mean pink, piggy eyes fixed on a quaking Jade.

Then the caretaker's gaze lifted and he took in the rest of the search party in the playground. 'Let's see, who else is involved in this latest little scam... Ah yes, Jimmy Black, Leonie Flowers, Daisy Morelli... the usual suspects!'

Daisy spoke up for the gang. 'We're only trying to find...'

'Save the excuses!' King boomed. 'I'll be making a note of all your names and passing them on to Mrs Waymann first thing in the morning.'

Wrroof-wrrooff! Lennox agreed.

Then the caretaker spotted Nathan. 'That doesn't include you, sonny. I know you can't possibly be mixed up with this hopeless lot.'

Nathan stared back, saying nothing but obviously thinking plenty.

What's going on inside that weird head? Daisy wondered.

'So go on, clear off!' King ordered.

Lennox dribbled and took a couple of steps forward.

There was no arguing with an overweight bulldog, so they retreated to the pavement outside the main gates.

'What now?' Jimmy asked impatiently. It was high time for him to be kicking a ball about in the park.

Leonie knitted her smooth brown eyebrows. 'Looks like we're stuck,' she muttered, shoving Midge's chocolate treat into her pocket. 'We'll just have to call off the search until tomorrow morning.'

Reluctantly, the others agreed, though Jade worried about Midge being out alone overnight and Kyle pointed out that every hour that went by was vital. Daisy sighed and admitted that there was nothing more they could do.

'Bye!' Jimmy said, the first to split. 'See ya!'

'Bye!' Jade and Kyle went off a different way.

'Sorry, Daisy,' Maya murmured for the hundredth time.

' 'Snot your fault. See you tomorrow.' She watched Maya and Leonie team up and head for home.

Which left her and Nathan standing by the school gate.

Daisy was about to beat a hasty retreat from the school nerd when Nathan said something really odd, even for him.

'So Daisy, how much does it mean to you to get Midge back in one piece?' His faded grey eyes stared at her, his voice was low and fast.

'Huh?' It took her a few seconds to realise that he was offering to do some kind of deal. 'Nathan, what's going on?'

'It's a simple question,' he insisted, squaring his shoulders and swaggering. 'I take it that the hamster means a lot to you?'

'Nathan, why are you coming across with this stupid gangster stuff?' Daisy's voice rose in protest. 'You can cut the American accent for a start!'

He shrugged and turned away. 'So, be like that.'

Daisy stepped across his path. 'No, sorry, Nathan. I didn't mean...' She gave in and decided to play it his way. 'OK, what's the deal?'

A faint smile played over Nathan's freckled face. 'The deal is, I get to join the gang.'

'*You?*' Daisy stepped back. The school geek, the maths and science genius, the kid who kept pet spiders, wanted to become one of them? 'Nathan, don't try to be funny!'

'I'm not laughing. I mean it, so you can close your mouth and stop gawping, Daisy Morelli.' Nathan snapped out his final demand. If Daisy didn't play it his way, he would simply turn his back and walk away. 'Listen, if you want to know what happened to the precious hamster, you have to let me join the gang!'

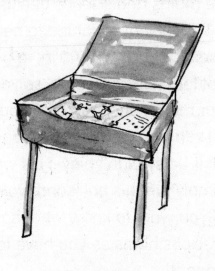

Eight

'That's blackmail!' Daisy protested. Suddenly she was seeing Nathan Moss in a new and chilly light.

'Yep,' he agreed.

'What are you saying? You know what happened to Midge?'

'Yep.'

'You've known all along?' Daisy's voice rose to a squeak.

'Yep.'

'What's more; you know where she is right this very minute?'

'You've got it,' Nathan confirmed. He let Legs out of his jar and up on to his shoulder.

'And you didn't say anything? You just let us all run around in circles looking for her, going crazy with worry?'

'Leonie and Jimmy shouldn't have ignored me,' he said coolly.

'If you want to blame anyone, blame them.'

Daisy thought back to the moment when the grand plan had collapsed. Maya had confessed that Midge had escaped, Leonie and Jimmy had sprinted out into the playground to try and catch her. And yes! She had a clear memory of weird Nathan standing by the netball post asking them what they were looking for.

'Back off, Nathan!' Leonie had yelled.

'Yeah, watch out!' Jimmy had cruised around him in a wide circle, looking anxiously for the missing pet.

'If they'd told me what they were doing, I could've helped,' he said calmly yet mysteriously.

Daisy let out a loud sigh. 'OK, give it to me straight, Nathan,' she said wearily.

'I saw it all,' he explained. 'I watched Maya take Midge from you and run to the bike shed. I watched Jimmy catch the cleaning-ball with Herbie inside. I heard Maya yell "ouch!" and drop the hamster. Midge made a bee-line for me. All I had to do was pick her up and pop her into Legs' jam-jar. Simple as that.'

'OK, you win. You can join the gang!' Daisy admitted defeat.

She was still reeling from the shock of Nathan's news when who should show up at the end of Woodbridge Road but Winona Jones.

All the more reason to keep things moving.

'So tell me where Midge is now!' Daisy begged.

'She's in a cardboard box inside my

classroom drawer,' Nathan told her, very
laid-back. He too had spotted Winona.

'C'mon, let's go and get her out of there!'
Daisy grabbed Nathan by the shirt sleeve
and tried to drag him towards the school.

But Nathan acted like they had all the time
in the world.

'Don't you owe a certain person an
apology first?'

'Not now. Later!' Daisy panicked at the
idea of having to eyeball Winona and tell her
everything. Tomorrow, face to face with Miss

Ambler would be soon enough for the Big Confession.

'Yoo-hoo, you two!' Winona waved at them. There was a bounce back in her stride and a gutsy look on her face. 'It's OK, I've been home and checked in with my mum. She gave me permission to come and join in the search for Midge!'

Daisy groaned as Winona drew near.

'Don't worry, we'll find her in the end,' Winona promised kindly, misunderstanding the reason behind Daisy's moan of despair. 'It stands to reason, a hamster can't just vanish into thin air!'

'Oh, Daisy!' The shock and hurt on Winona's face when she heard the full confession was difficult to bear.

'I'm sorry!' Daisy whispered.

Nightmare! How had it all gone so wrong? Was this her just reward for being mean to Winona? Did the universe really operate in that organised a way?

Nathan stood by with an air of quiet satisfaction, while Legs took a stroll across his chest. 'Maybe Winona would like to join the gang as well,' he suggested.

Daisy gulped, then turned to Winona. 'Would you?'

Winona's blue eyes shone. A dream come true. 'Could I *really*?'

Daisy nodded. 'On one condition.'

'Which is?'

'You have to learn to be bad. I mean, really, really bad!' As Leonie had said, "No more Saint Winona!"

'You mean, like you?' Winona considered the challenge. 'I'd have to do horrible stuff with superglue and secret notes; that kind of thing?'

Daisy nodded. 'What d'you think? Can you do it?'

Winona took a deep breath then came up with her answer. 'I could try!'

'Mr King, is it OK if Nathan, Daisy and I slip

back into the classroom, please?' Winona started as she meant to continue from now on by wheedling her way past the school janitor.

'What for?' came the gruff, grunting reply. Fat Lennox sat wheezily to heel outside his master's damp basement office.

'Erm, we just forgot something important,' Winona told him.

'It's way past home time,' Bernie pointed out, his eyes narrowing suspiciously. 'I've already told Daisy Morelli to make herself scarce.'

Winona ignored the Daisy remark. 'We thought we'd better ask your permission, Mr King,' she said sweetly. 'Nathan needs to collect his trumpet for Music Centre. I have to pick up a book for my English homework and Daisy – er, Daisy needs something from her drawer.'

King sniffed grudgingly. 'You and Nathan can go ahead, no problem. But I wouldn't trust Daisy Morelli as far as I could throw her.'

So Winona and Nathan had to leave Daisy sulking by the main door while they went into the deserted school to rescue Midge from Nathan's drawer.

'It's not fair!' Daisy muttered to herself, all the events of the day had been building to this point, and now, just because of Bernie-the-Bully King's suspicious mind, she was forced to miss it.

But wait! She remembered the french window leading into the classroom from the playground. If she scooted around and knocked on the window, Nathan and Winona would be able to let her in. She would be in on the finale after all.

So she sprinted around corners, ducking low past Bernie King's office, ignoring Lennox's throaty growl. And she arrived at the french window just in time to see Winona and Nathan enter the classroom by the more usual route.

'Psst!' She hissed, then tapped lightly at the window.

Winona spotted her and immediately opened the glass door.

'Good thinking, Daisy!'

'So, c'mon, Nathan, open your drawer!' Daisy was impatient to see Midge with her own eyes.

But he took his time, whisking his hands in front of the drawer like a magician about to draw a rabbit out of a top-hat. 'Da-dah!' he cried, then slid the drawer out of its slot.

Empty!

Well, actually, full of chewed paper and wax crayons and a wrecked cardboard box with hamster teeth-marks all over it.

But no actual hamster.

'Oh!' Winona peered inside the drawer in dismay.

Nathan leaned forward and pulled out one semi-digested maths project. He studied it in horror. 'Ambler will kill me!' he breathed.

'OK, Einstein, what now?' Daisy stood with her hands on her hips, demanding the next genius-move.

All three stood for a while in silent dismay.

Then Daisy heard a squeaking, creaking, trundling noise from the window sill.

Squeak-squeak, creak-creak, trundle-trundle.

The sound of a hamster using an exercise wheel.

'Midge!' they cried, and dashed to the hamster's cage.

The door was open and a cloud of dusty wood shavings was being raised as the exercise wheel spun round.

Squeak-squeak-squeak! The wheel turned. And a small, furry face peered out at the astonished trio.

'Midge, you're safe! You found your own way back!' Winona breathed.

Creak-creak! The hamster trundled on.

'Nice one, Midge!' Nathan grunted. 'But what about my maths project?'

Daisy just grinned and thought of what she would tell the gang.

Trundle-trundle.

Space station commander to crew. Midge returned to base.

Mission accomplished. I repeat, mission accomplished!

Look out for more
Definitely Daisy adventures...

You must be joking, Jimmy!
Jenny Oldfield

It's school sports day and Jimmy happens upon his teacher's diary. Daisy expects to learn spicy secrets, but the diary, like Miss Ambler, is DULL! So Daisy 'invents' more exciting entries. Now Jimmy believes that Rambler-Ambler is going out with a soccer superstar. 'No way!' his classmates cry. Can Daisy get them to believe...

I'd like a little word, Leonie!

Jenny Oldfield

It's World Book Day, and Daisy's class
dress up as book characters. Leonie's
really into it – until she sees nerdy
Nathan wearing the same outfit as her.
But when she messes up an important task
for Miss Boring-Snoring, Daisy twigs that
their twin cat costumes could be a way
out of trouble for golden girl, Leonie...

Not now, Nathan!
Jenny Oldfield

Nerdy Nathan's pet spider has gone
missing. Daisy and the gang carry out a
frantic search, but they fail to find crafty
Legs. Poor Nathan's worried sick. But
scatty Miss Ambler, busy rehearsing for
Thursday's school concert, has no time to
waste on a pesky runaway pet...

What's the matter, Maya?

Jenny Oldfield

Shock, horror... Bernie King discovers deep holes in the school soccer pitch! When the angry caretaker accuses an innocent dog, only shy Maya knows that he's covering up for his own pet. But she's too scared to tell on Fat Lennox. Can Daisy discover the real culprit?